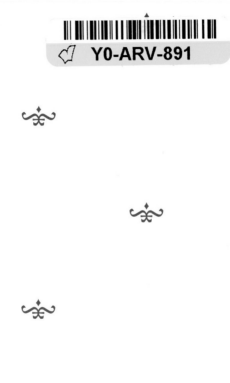

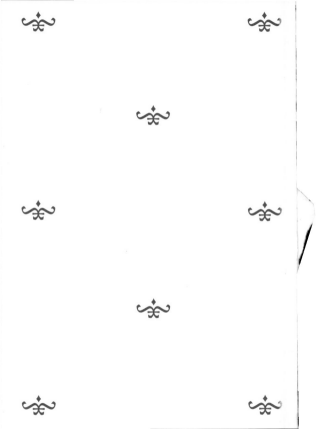

A GOLFER'S
12 DAYS OF
Christmas

SUE CARABINE

Gibbs Smith, Publisher
Salt Lake City

First Edition
10 09 08 07 06 05   5 4 3 2 1

Published by
Gibbs Smith, Publisher
P.O. Box 667
Layton, Utah 84041

1-800-748-5439 orders
www.gibbs-smith.com

Designed and produced by Dawn DeVries Sokol
Printed and bound in China

ISBN 1-58685-828-9

On the 1st day of
CHRISTMAS,
Todd tallied
up his score.

"I need that hole in one,"
he mused, and headed
for the door.

—⁓—

"I'll leave right now
	and play a round to reach
	MY LIFELONG DREAM."

On the course he vowed,
"I'll use this club and
	make it on this green!"

He lined up his shot,
addressed the ball, and
swinging, yelled, "OKAY!"

But a tree and nest took
Todd's *great* hit as a
partridge flew away.

On the 2nd day of
CHRISTMAS,
Todd vowed to try again,

He'd hit that perfect shot
today in ONE instead of ten.

He gazed out at the fairway
and picked out his
FAVORITE wood,

Again he swung with
all his *might.* "That," he yelled,
"LOOKS GOOD!"

No sooner had he said
those words when he heard
a frightened scream,

He'd SURPRISED two
lovebirds **holding hands**
behind a bush, it seems.

"**SO** sorry, didn't see you there," said Todd, who felt *quite small,*

"I've GOT to score **a hole in one**," and, stooping, grabbed his ball.

On the 3rd day of
CHRISTMAS,
Todd said, *"I'll not give up.*

Today, I'll concentrate *so* hard,
I know I'll have
GOOD LUCK!"

He *teed off*, and then
bogeyed one, was
SET TO HIT ONCE MORE

When he saw three ladies on the course, so Todd yelled loudly,

"FORE!"

They smiled and waved but
didn't move. Were these
three IN A TRANCE?

Todd marched right up to
lecture them and learned
they were from France.

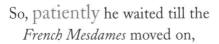

So, patiently he waited till the
French Mesdames moved on,

"Today," he *glumly* thought
out loud, "there'll be no
hole in one!"

On the *4th* day of
CHRISTMAS,
Todd woke up with a **start**,

"Today is going to be
        THE DAY.
    I feel it in my *heart*."

Blasting from the bunker,
he was proud of his
GREAT shot.

He did *quite* well till someone
yelled, "Today, man,
I'm SO hot!"

This guy would not
stop boasting, and being
VERY wordy,

He put Todd's concentration off
by LOUDLY calling, ***"Birdie!"***

FOUR TIMES MORE

the guy had chortled this

same *irritating* cry.

"Say 'birdie' one more time," Todd *growled*, "and I promise you, you'll DIE!"

On the *5th* day of

CHRISTMAS,

bleary Todd was
wound up *TIGHT*,

The previous day
        had been *so* bad, he
                didn't sleep ALL night.

"*Today* I'll take my lucky iron,
    my rabbit's foot and keys,

A golf ball signed by
  TIGER WOODS, and
    my five *golden* tees.

It's got to be my *lucky* day, but
I'm **NOT** superstitious,

I'll try hard not to KNOCK
on wood or folks will be
SUSPICIOUS!"

Maybe it was *lack of faith*,
perhaps LUCK just worked
for some,

—〰—

But Todd soon left the
golf course with a
countenance **quite glum!**

On the *6th* day of

CHRISTMAS,

Todd traveled to the course,

He SIGHED, "I'll take it *easy*,
and my golf strokes won't be
FORCED."

He hit the ball with **confidence**,
made par with each
smooth stroke,

Until he reached the
18th hole where his dream
WENT UP IN SMOKE.

The ball **FLEW OFF** the
fairway and—*Alas!*—a man
it pegged.

Todd ran over to apologize, saw
a **GOOSE EGG** on his head.

On the *7th* day of
CHRISTMAS,
lightning flashed
and thunder *clapped*,

But Todd was **STILL**
determined as he *jumped*
out of the sack.

Not rain,
nor snow, nor sleet,
nor hail,
whatever came along,

Would keep him from his
DESTINY to make
a hole in one!

He made it to the 9TH HOLE where the ball rolled in the pond,

But his level of frustration wasn't like the *IRATE* swans!

On the 8th day of
CHRISTMAS,

Todd's goal was *still* in sight,

He'd dreamed about his
Christmas wish. "*Today* things
feel **just** right."

Groundskeepers were out
mowing as greens GLISTENED,
damp with dew,

When **Todd** donned his
    new golfing gloves, he *heard* a
strange sound: **"MOO!"**

Well, *right there* near the golf
course stood UNHAPPY dairy cows

Todd thought, "They ALL need
milking. Is there someone
I can rouse?"

He climbed the fence, and
then he tried **IN VAIN** to
move them on.

Again his plans were thwarted
to achieve his HOLE IN ONE!

—⁓—

On the *9th* day of

CHRISTMAS,

with his putter in his bag,

Todd whistled as he
    drove along—he'd not let
        his spirits *sag*.

Arriving at the first tee,
he hit a powerful stroke,

The ball flew **LONG** and
out of bounds, landed near
some *girlish* folk.

As they listened to their iPods,
they **DANCED** lightheartedly,

Oblivious to the golf game that
Todd played so *seriously*.

"Would you gals find
somewhere **ELSE** to dance?"
Todd asked them
pleasantly,

But with music POUNDING
in their ears, they
danced INCESSANTLY.

On the *10th* day of
CHRISTMAS,
Todd took Ken Lord along.

Perhaps he'd pick up
from his friend what he was
doing WRONG.

Todd **followed** Ken's
suggestions as they went from
hole to hole,

Still *hoping* with each
golf stroke he would finally reach
his GOAL.

While playing at the *15th* hole
and soaking up the sun,

Todd saw his friend a-leaping—
Ken had made
A HOLE IN ONE!

On the *11th* day of
CHRISTMAS,

Todd vowed to try *once more*

And not get SO discouraged
after yesterday's *sad* score.

But arriving at the
golf club he was
SHOCKED to see the greens:

*Men were digging up the sprinkler
pipes and working on the sleeves.*

"HOW LONG will these men work today and when can I *return?*"

Todd asked the head groundskeeper, who was looking *rather stern*.

"*The* course is closed
ALL day today,
the pipes need some repair.

These plumbers **need** to
do their job and don't like
us to STARE."

So on the 12th day of
CHRISTMAS,
fresh from a *dream-free* night,

TODD quickly donned his
old golf gear and set out at
first light.

He gazed out o'er the golf
course, **LOVED** the start
of a *new* day.

Instead of worrying SO much,
he'd just go out and play.

From the 1st hole through
the 17th, he'd been having
SO MUCH FUN;

And then driving to the
18th hole, Todd got his
hole in one!

FROM A DISTANCE he
could hear the local high school
band *on cue*;

The drummers drummed
as if to say, "Todd, we're
SO PROUD OF YOU!"

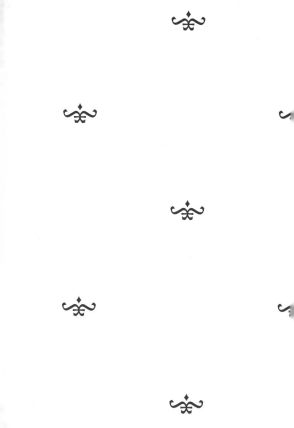

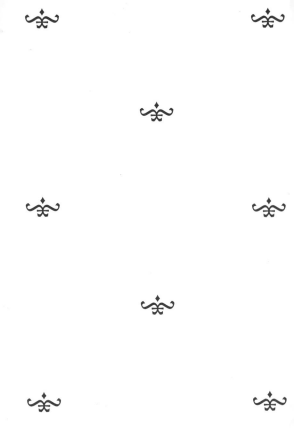